PAUL GERAGHTY

THE HOPPAMELEON

For Careoleeine and frog-lovers shorter than a table

This paperback edition first published in 2013 by Andersen Press Ltd.,
20 Vauxhall Bridge Road, London SW1V 2SA.
Published in Australia by Random House Australia Pty.,
Level 3, 100 Pacific Highway, North Sydney, NSW 2060.
First published in Great Britain in 2001 by Hutchinson.
Copyright © Paul Geraghty, 2001.
The rights of Paul Geraghty to be identified as
the author and illustrator of this work have
been asserted by him in accordance with the
Copyright, Designs and Patents Act, 1988.
All rights reserved.
Printed and bound in Singapore by Tien Wah Press.

10 9 8 7 6 5 4 3 2 1

British Library Cataloguing in Publication Data available.
ISBN 978 1 84939 773 5

Long before you were born, when the world was still quite young, there was a sleepy, slurpy swamp. And as the dozy insects buzzed above the water, a very odd-looking creature swam below.

Then, its beautiful eyes popped up.

The world was filled with colour. So out hopped the creature, all green and glossy, and started to chirp, "Calling anyone like me! I'm looking for a friend! Calling anyone like me!"

When something tasty landed nearby, the chirping stopped. Its huge mouth opened, and out shot a long, sticky tongue . . .

. . . which hit another long, sticky tongue. "Who do you think you are," bellowed the chameleon, "trying to steal my dinner?" "I-I don't know," said the very odd-looking creature. "I'm just looking for a friend. Who do *you* think I am?"

"Well," the chameleon grumbled, "you catch food with a long, sticky tongue like mine and I'm a chameleon, so you must be some kind of chameleon too. Now hop it. This is *my* patch!"

"Then I'm a chameleon," chirped the very odd-looking creature, "because I can hunt like a chameleon. And I'm just looking for a chameleon friend."

"But you're hopping just like I do," said a grasshopper, "so you must be some kind of grasshopper too."

"You're right," said the very odd-looking creature.

"In that case, I must be a *hoppa*meleon." And with a splash, it dived back into the swamp.

"Blooble-blooble, I'm a hoppameleon," blurbled the very odd-looking creature, "because I can hop like a grasshopper and hunt like a chameleon. And I'm just looking for a hoppameleon friend."

"But you can swim like I do," bubbled a passing turtle,
"so you must be some kind of turtle too."
"Then I must be a *turtle*hoppameleon!" sang the very
odd-looking creature, leaping from the water . . .

. . . and splashing a thirsty parrot.

"Hey!" yelled the parrot. "Who do you think you are, splashing my drink all over me?"

"I'm a turtlehoppameleon," sang the very odd-looking creature, "because I can swim like a turtle, hop like a grasshopper, and hunt like a chameleon. And I'm just looking for a turtlehoppameleon friend."

"But you can chirp like I do," said the parrot, who had stopped drinking,
"so you must be some kind of parrot too."
"Then I must be a *parrot*turtlehoppameleon!"
announced the very odd-looking
creature, bounding off . . .

. . . and landing beside a stealthy lizard.

"Woah!" yelled the lizard. "Who do you think you are, frightening away my food like that?"

"I'm a parroturtlehoppameleon," explained the very odd-looking creature, "because I can chirp like a parrot, swim like a turtle, hop like a grasshopper, and hunt like a chameleon. And I'm just looking for a parroturtlehoppameleon friend."

"But you cling with padded feet just like mine," said the lizard,
"so you must be some kind of lizard too."
"Well, then I must be a *lizzy*parroturtlehoppameleon,"
exclaimed the very odd-looking creature,

"because I can cling like a lizard, chirp like a parrot, swim like a
turtle, hop like a grasshopper, and hunt like a chameleon. And
I'm just looking for a lizzyparroturtlehoppameleon friend."

"But you have beautiful big eyes like mine," interrupted a bushbaby, "so you must be some kind of bushbaby too!"

"Then I must surely be a *baby*lizzyparroturtlehoppameleon,"
said the very odd-looking creature, almost out of breath,
'because I can see like a bushbaby, cling like a lizard,
chirp like a parrot, swim like a turtle, hop like a
grasshopper, and hunt like a chameleon."

"And that must be the longest name in the whole of the animal kingdom." The very odd-looking creature sighed. "But I would swap all of my names just for *one* friend."

Next hop, the very odd-looking creature landed right
in front of another just like itself.
"I'm a babylizzyparroturtlehoppameleon!"
said the very odd-looking creature. "What are you?"
The other one looked for a moment, then opened its huge mouth and said . . .

"*So am I!* Let's go hopping together!"
And off they bounced, their rubbery feet making a most peculiar *Frog! Frog! Frog!* noise on the lily pads as they went.

Babylizzyparroturtlehoppameleons later got a much shorter name, but I can't for the life of me remember what that name is, or where it came from. Can you?

OTHER BOOKS BY
PAUL GERAGHTY

9781849393881

9781849393768

9781849395632

9781849390279

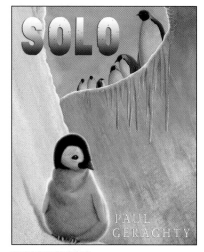

9781849392440

9781849395571